P9-BIN-294

Published by the Royal Ontario Museum with the generous support of the Louise Hawley Stone Charitable Trust

For Justin, and all the adventures that await you

D. D.

For Rowan and Maxwel

T. W.

Royal Ontario Museum 100 Queen's Park Toronto, Ontario M5S 2C6
www.rom.on.ca

Project Director: Glen Ellis   Design: Tara Winterhalt

Library and Archives Canada Cataloguing in Publication

Dias, Denise
Burton & Isabelle Pipistrelle : out of the bat cave / Denise Dias ; illustrated by Tara Winterhalt.

ISBN 978-0-88854-485-8

1. Bats–Juvenile fiction. I. Winterhalt, Tara II. Title.
III. Title: Burton & Isabelle Pipistrelle. IV. Title: Out of the bat cave.

PS8607.I26B87 2011   jC813'.6   C2011-906118-X

Printed and bound in Canada by Friesens Printers, Altona, Manitoba.
The Royal Ontario Museum is an agency of the Government of Ontario.

BURTON & ISABELLE
PIPISTRELLE

BURTON & ISABELLE
PIPISTRELLE

out of the bat cave

Denise Dias

illustrated by

Tara Winterhalt

ROM
Royal Ontario Museum Press

In a deep, dark, and damp cave, where the drip-drops of water sound like music and rough rocks hang like works of art, a family of Pipistrelle bats gathered to make their roost.

The Pipistrelles had yellowish and brownish fur that was fluffed up around their ears. They flew like dancing butterflies.

They were a tiny bunch of bats and the tiniest of them all was a bat named Burton.

Burton wasn't like the other Pipistrelles who always stuck together. He had a curious mind and a brave heart.

Burton usually poked around the roost when the other bats were off hunting for insects or fast asleep upside-down. He liked to stay up late in the mornings, daydreaming of new caves and hollow trees to explore.

Every night, Isabelle said, "Hurry up, Burton! There will be no bugs left!"

And when the black night melted into day, she hissed, "Get to bed, Burton! The sun will be up soon!"

Isabelle followed all the rules and was always on her best behaviour.

One foggy night, while all the bats were out scanning trees and skimming
ponds for a delicious dinner, Burton noticed something strange.

A small stream of light poured into the cave from behind a puzzle of rocks.
It's not morning yet, thought Burton. *But what else could it be?* Confused but
curious, he decided to take a closer look . . .

He squeaked, shrieked, and screeched at the beam of light.
The Pipistrelles use *echolocation* to locate and identify things
by listening to the echoes of their own calls.

But all Burton could hear was the echoing sing-song sounds
of the water in the cave.

So he decided to squeeze his furry little body right through
the narrow wet rocks until he popped out the other side.

GAL
BIRD

The Bat Cave | La Grotte des

Looking around with his tiny heart pounding—BA-BOOM, BA-BOOM—
Burton sat frozen in fear and wonder. *Maybe I should turn back,* he thought.
What would Isabelle say about this?

But he took a deep breath, stretched his wings wide, and charged ahead
with all his might.

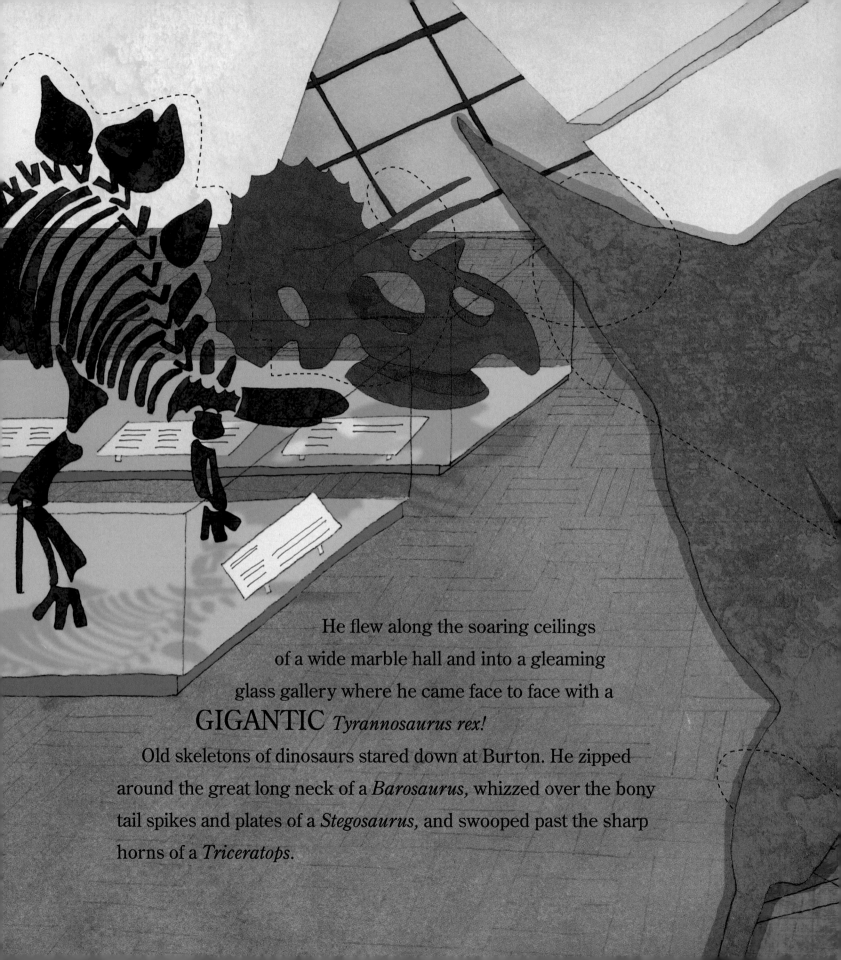

He flew along the soaring ceilings
of a wide marble hall and into a gleaming
glass gallery where he came face to face with a
GIGANTIC *Tyrannosaurus rex!*
Old skeletons of dinosaurs stared down at Burton. He zipped
around the great long neck of a *Barosaurus,* whizzed over the bony
tail spikes and plates of a *Stegosaurus,* and swooped past the sharp
horns of a *Triceratops.*

He imagined a world where dinosaurs stomped around
and roamed free, more than 65 million years ago!

He fluttered into another gallery that looked
just like an old pirate's buried treasure. Shiny cases
and chests of drawers were loaded with pretty gems,
precious pieces of gold, minerals, and even meteorite specimens!

He was fascinated by the sparkle of deep blue sapphires,
crystal clear diamonds, and sea-green emeralds.

I've never seen rocks like this before, thought Burton.
Isabelle will never believe this!

Burton found a quiet gallery that was filled with glittery ball gowns, delicate gloves, and fine silk dresses displayed next to bright puffy jackets and embroidered suits.

He dove into the sleeve of a soft coat and pretended to be a powerful prince. He wrapped himself in a heavy purple dress and imagined he was swimming in an ocean of grape juice. He curled up inside a lace glove and thought he was trapped in a spider's web!

With all the excitement, Burton completely lost track of time. It was almost morning and the sun was starting to rise.

There was much more to explore but he had to get home! Burton turned to make his way back to the roost, but he wasn't sure which way to go. He frantically flew through all the same twists and turns but it was no use—he was lost!

With each passing minute, Burton grew more frightened . . . *What would Isabelle do?*

Suddenly, he remembered—echolocation! He let out a few small shrieks and heard them bounce back. But none of the echoes sounded familiar.

Burton nervously flew left and right, up and down, side to side, and around and again! How would he ever find his way back home?

Tired and terrified, he collapsed in the vast silence of the empty space around him.

I wish Isabelle were here, he thought.

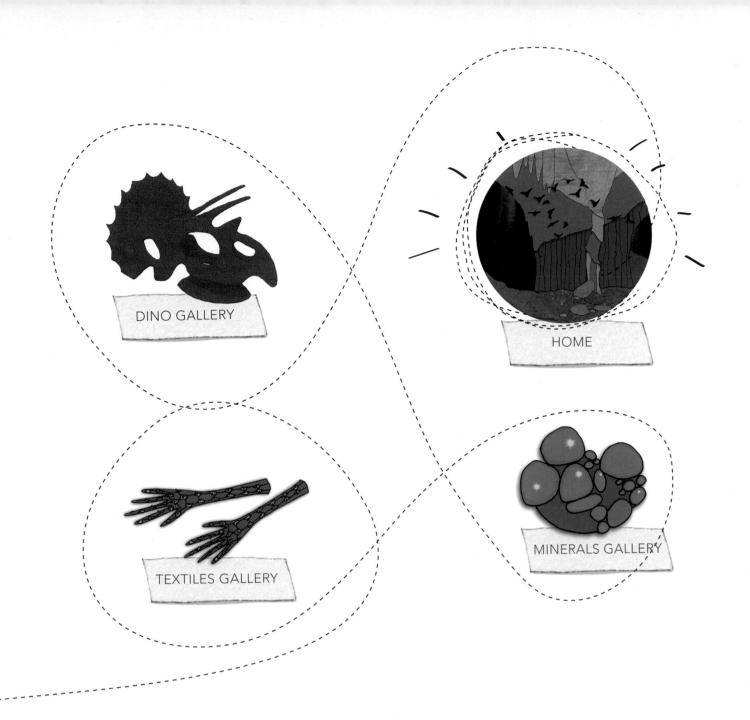

DINO GALLERY

HOME

TEXTILES GALLERY

MINERALS GALLERY

Just when the morning light was breaking through the night sky, he heard a faint, faraway, and familiar drip-drop. YES! Burton recognized the watery string of sound from the cave and triumphantly sang a sequence of calls that echoed through the galleries. He navigated the invisible map of drip-drop echoes back to the Pipistrelle roost.

He slid his way back through the narrow rocks and hurried into the
cave just as all the Pipistrelles were dashing in from their nocturnal hunt.

"Burton! Where have you been?!" asked Isabelle. He eagerly told
her about his amazing adventure and all the dinosaurs, treasures, and
costumes he had discovered.

"Oh, Burton, you really let your imagination run wild this time!" laughed Isabelle. "When will you stop daydreaming and start behaving?"

For a second, Burton wondered if he had imagined the whole wonderful night in the museum. As he settled upside-down for the day, he could hardly wait for the next nightfall to find out.

BAT FACTS

with Dr. Lim

1. Bats are not blind. In fact, they can see better at night than humans (but humans have better daytime vision and can see colours better).

2. Most bats have echolocation, a sonar system that helps them to fly in the dark and "see with their ears."

3. Bats are the only mammals that can fly.

4. The bones of a bat's wing are like the bones of a human hand —the bones in the wing are like the long "finger" bones, and the little claw on the wing is a "thumb."

5. Bats can eat from 50% to more than 100% of their body weight in insects each night.

Dr. Burton Lim is Assistant Curator, Mammalogy, at the ROM.

Burton's adventure takes place at the Royal Ontario Museum (ROM) in Toronto, Ontario, Canada. The galleries he discovers are the James and Louise Temerty Galleries of the Age of Dinosaurs, the Teck Suite of Galleries: Earth's Treasures, and the Patricia Harris Gallery of Textiles & Costume.